Part III of the "Read, then Read More" Series

The Box

Written by Lisa and Dallas Lewis

Illustrated by Dallas Lewis

"I'm bored!" mumbled Juan.

"I'm bored too," said Silly Billy.

Juan and Silly Billy thought that they had done everything there was to do in the whole city. They had watched their favorite scary video tape more than two hundred times. They had played their most favorite computer games over and over until they could hardly move their fingers. They watched Silly Billy's dog, Hollywood, fly through the air. But, even that bored them now.

"Let's get Hollywood to fly next to the air-planes again. That always scares the pilots," Juan said.

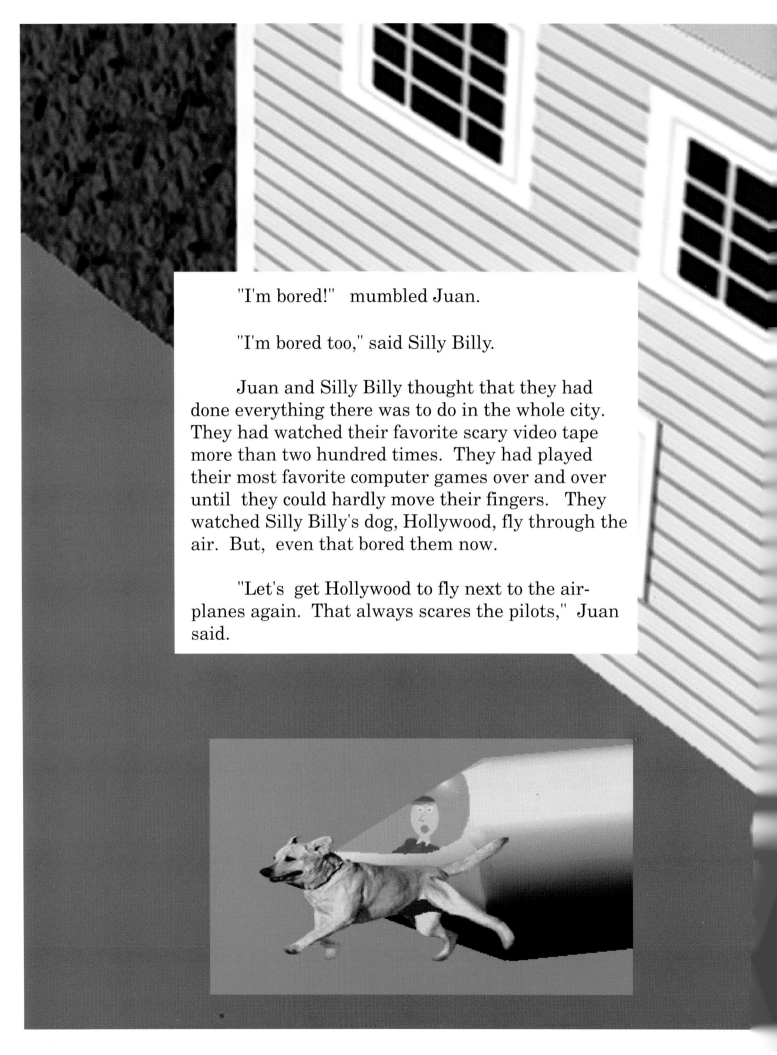

"I don't think so. My Mom told me not to let him do that anymore. Hey look! Here comes Big Filmore," Silly Billy said, as Big Filmore strolled down the sidewalk.

    "Hi, you guys," Big Filmore said.

    "Big Filmore, can we go play in your barn?" Juan asked.

    Big Filmore replied, "Sorry, but we can't. My Dad has been in there for the last three weeks. He won't come out."

    Silly Billy asked, "What's he doing in there?"

    Big Filmore told them, "He's been in there ever since he learned how to read. We saw him with a big stack of books and a computer. We haven't seen him since. My Mom is really worried about him.

Big Filmore asked, "Hey, where's Barb-a-barb-a-bab-a-dad? I thought that she was going to meet us here today."

Silly Billy commanded, "Call her, Hollywood!"

Hollywood howled, and out of the blue came Barb's spaceship.

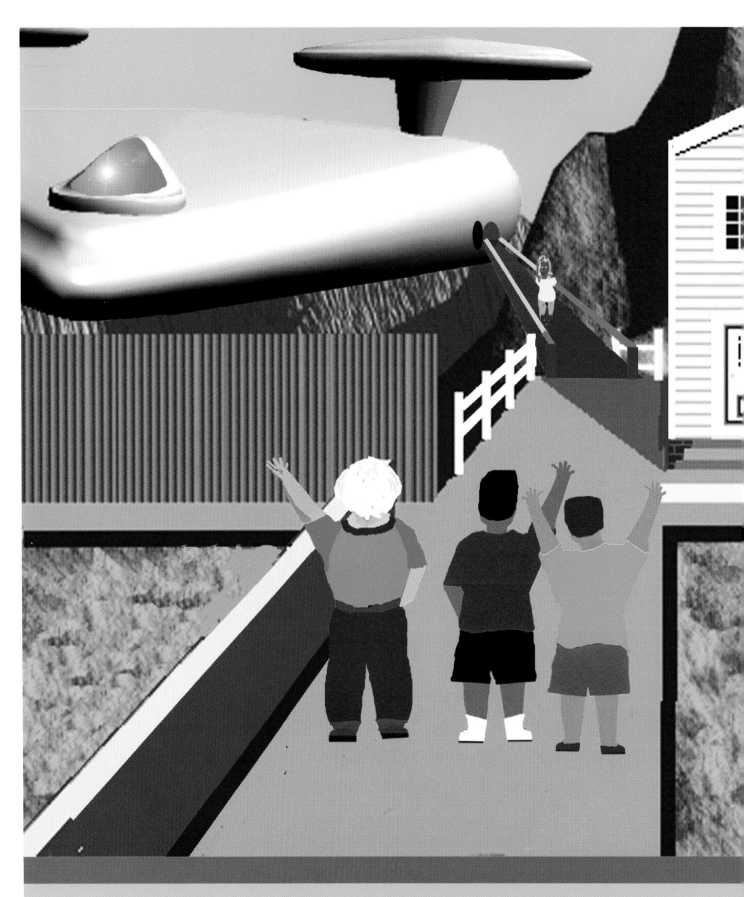

The space ship landed with a slight s-w-o-o-s-h in Silly Billy's back yard. It was sparkling and shiny - brand new.

"Barb-a-barb-a-bab-a-dad! You've got a new ship!" Silly Billy said, as he ran to meet her.

As Barb said hello to Silly Billy and Big Filmore, she noticed that Juan didn't seem very happy. "What's wrong with you, Juan?" she asked. "You look pretty upset."

"I'm bored. There's nothing to do," Juan complained.

"Bored? You need to fill your head with new ideas. Have you read any books lately?" Barb asked.

"Books?" Juan replied.

"Whenever you get bored, read something," Barb said. "The more you read, the less boxed in you will be."

"What do you mean by boxed in?" Juan asked.

Barb said, "Check this out! My new ship has a little gizmo on it that will show you just what I mean."

Big Filmore, Silly Billy, Juan and Barb-a-barb-a-bab-a-dad all got into Barb's new ship, and off they zoomed. Barb had a special viewing screen, like a big television, that dropped out of her control panel.

"Watch this!" Barb said as she flipped a switch.

On Barb's screen, they could see lots of streets and rows of houses. Some people sat on their steps and others stood on sidewalks. After Barb flipped the switch, they could see little boxes around many of the people.

"What are all of those little yellow boxes?"   Juan asked.

Barb answered, "The boxes show the limits of their imaginations."

"My Mom says that this isn't a very good side of town. I bet that's why their boxes are so small," Juan said, pointing to the people on the screen.

Barb zoomed in on a different group of houses. None of the people had boxes at all.

"Look!" Big Filmore said, "There's Tony, Sara and their Mom. Where are their boxes?"

Barb inquired, " Does their family read much?"

"Yeah!" Juan said, "Tony's Mom reads them stories every night. They love to read, even on their own."

"There is your answer, Juan. The more you read, the more imagination you have. Reading gets you out of The Box," Barb told them.

Barb's spaceship zoomed over downtown. They could see lots of business people wearing suits and ties, and hustling up and down the streets. Barb flipped her switch again. Many of them had boxes around them too.

"Look!" Silly Billy shouted, "There is Mr. Twinkwinkler. Look at his box! My Dad says that he's one of the richest people in town. How can he be so rich, and still have a box?"

Barb replied, "Sure, some people have lots of money, but they only read about how to make more money. Their greed keeps them boxed in, too. That's why so many people with money are so unhappy."

"But what about us, Barb? Can you put that camera on us so we can see if we have boxes?" Big Filmore asked.

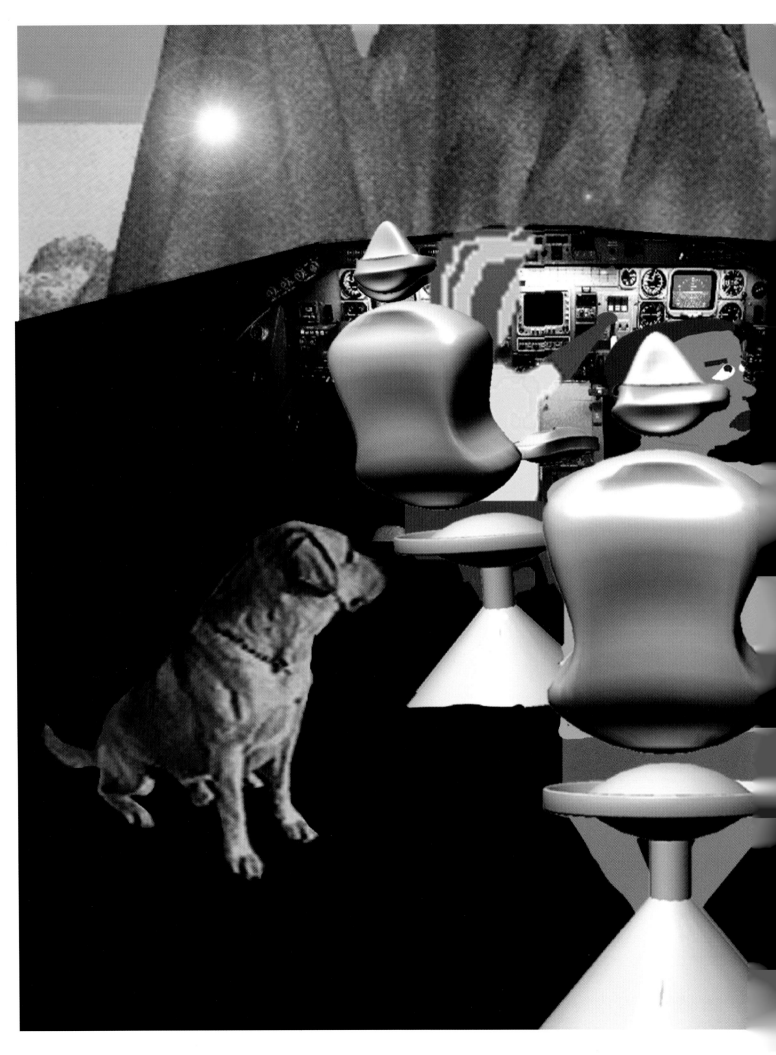

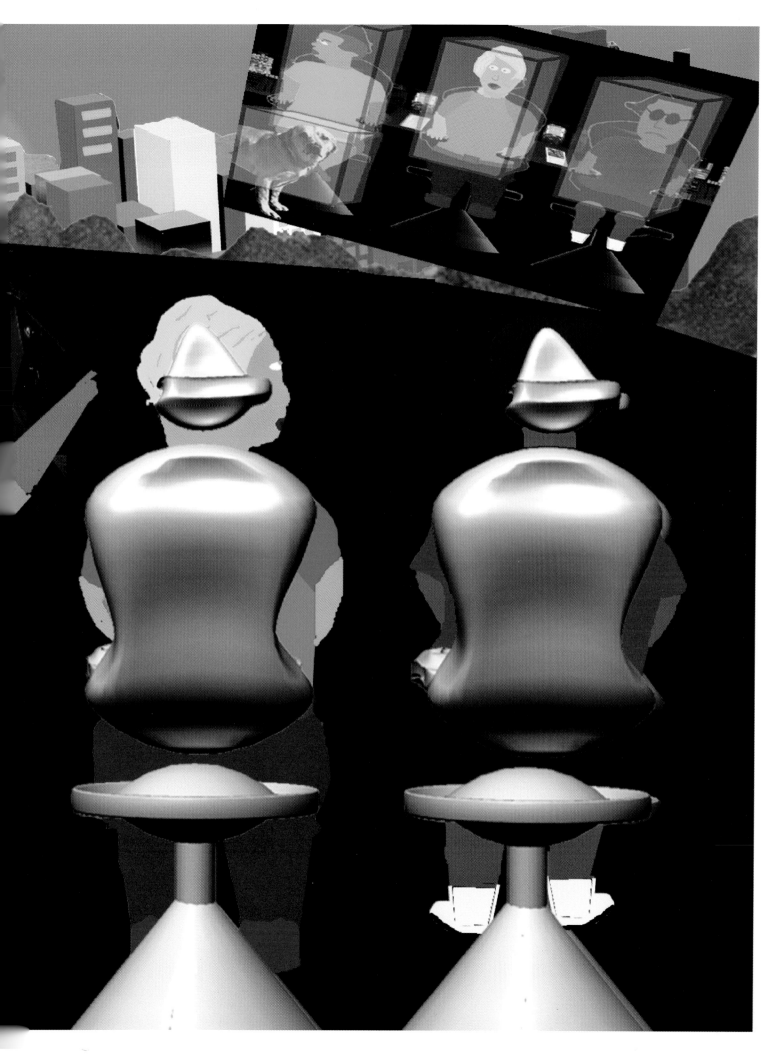

Barb pushed some buttons and the big computer screen showed all four of the kids. Each of them had a box except for Barb-a-barb-a-bab-a-dad.

"What are we going to do? We all have boxes!" The boys groaned.

She said, "Just read! That's all you have to do. Reading always gives me new ideas. That is why I don't get boxed in. Reading will do the same for you."

The spaceship zoomed all over town. Finally it returned to Big Filmore's neighborhood. They could see Big Filmore's farm, house and barn. On Barb's screen, they watched the barn door swing open and Mr. Filmore walked out.

Big Filmore said, "There's my Dad. He's finally coming out of the barn. Look, you guys! He doesn't have a box at all."

The spaceship landed, and they all jumped out to see what Mr. Filmore was doing. He stood in the barn-yard, looking off into space. The boys and Hollywood approached him carefully.

"Dad! Dad! What's wrong?" Big Filmore asked, as they helped him to find a seat beside the barn.

He said, "I don't believe it. I just don't believe it."

Big Filmore asked, "Believe what, Dad?"

He responded, "There is so much I don't know. I read about the thousands of inventions made in ancient Africa, India, China, South America and Europe. I visited all of them, using the Internet."

Then he added, "I read about the history of women, cars, math and science. I've learned so much that I feel like a new man. And I learned how to use computers to learn even more stuff. I used to hate computers. Now, I think I'm going to start a computer business."

They all walked into the barn. They were surrounded by computers.

Mr. Filmore said, "You kids are so lucky. I'm 48 years old and I just learned how to read. There are millions of people all over the world who can't read. Each of you can read.   There is so much ahead of you to explore, if you would just use your brains and imaginations."

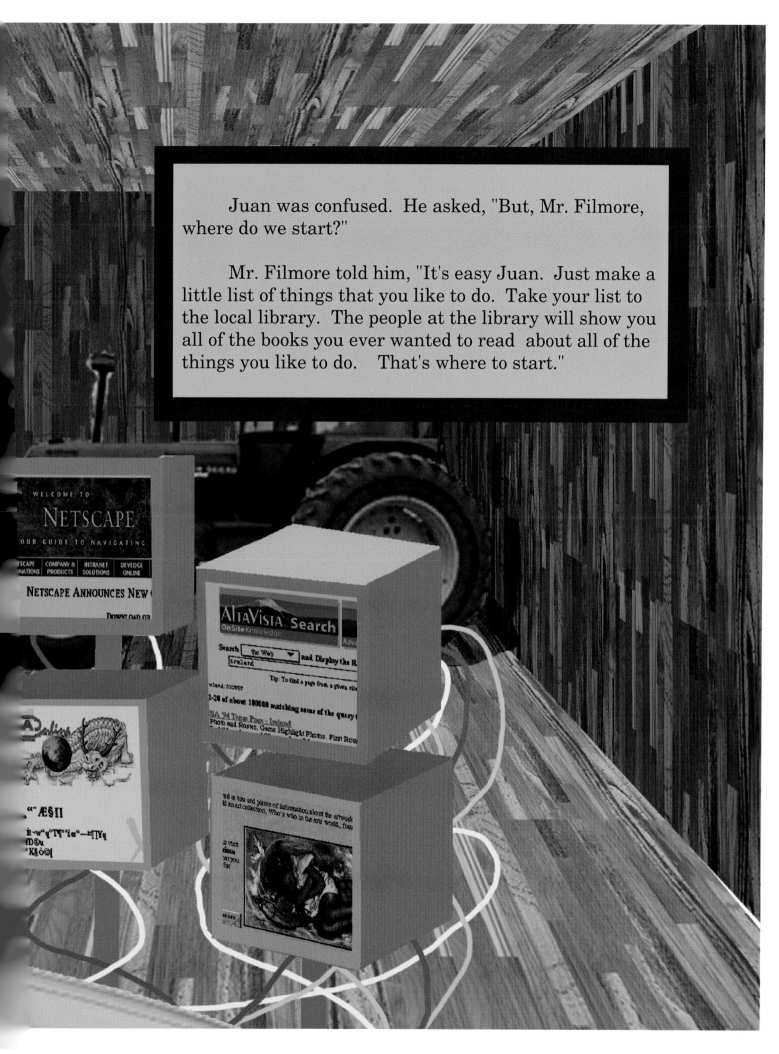

Juan was confused. He asked, "But, Mr. Filmore, where do we start?"

Mr. Filmore told him, "It's easy Juan. Just make a little list of things that you like to do. Take your list to the local library. The people at the library will show you all of the books you ever wanted to read about all of the things you like to do.   That's where to start."

"But Dad," Big Filmore pleaded, "what are all of these computers for?"

Mr. Filmore replied, "They are for the Internet, son. On the Internet, I visit libraries. I talk to people from all over the world. Sometimes I just play games."

"Can we visit some libraries, Mr. Filmore?" Juan asked.

Mr. Filmore's eyes began to sparkle, "Let's go! Let's boot up the computers!"

Big Filmore, Juan, Silly Billy, Barb-a-barb-a-bab-a-dad and even Hollywood surfed the Net for hours. They read, looked at pictures, listened to music and had lots of fun.

Barb had to go home. She said her goodbyes, hopped into her spaceship and zoomed away.

"Let's see if this box - viewer - thing still works," Barb said, as she zipped off.

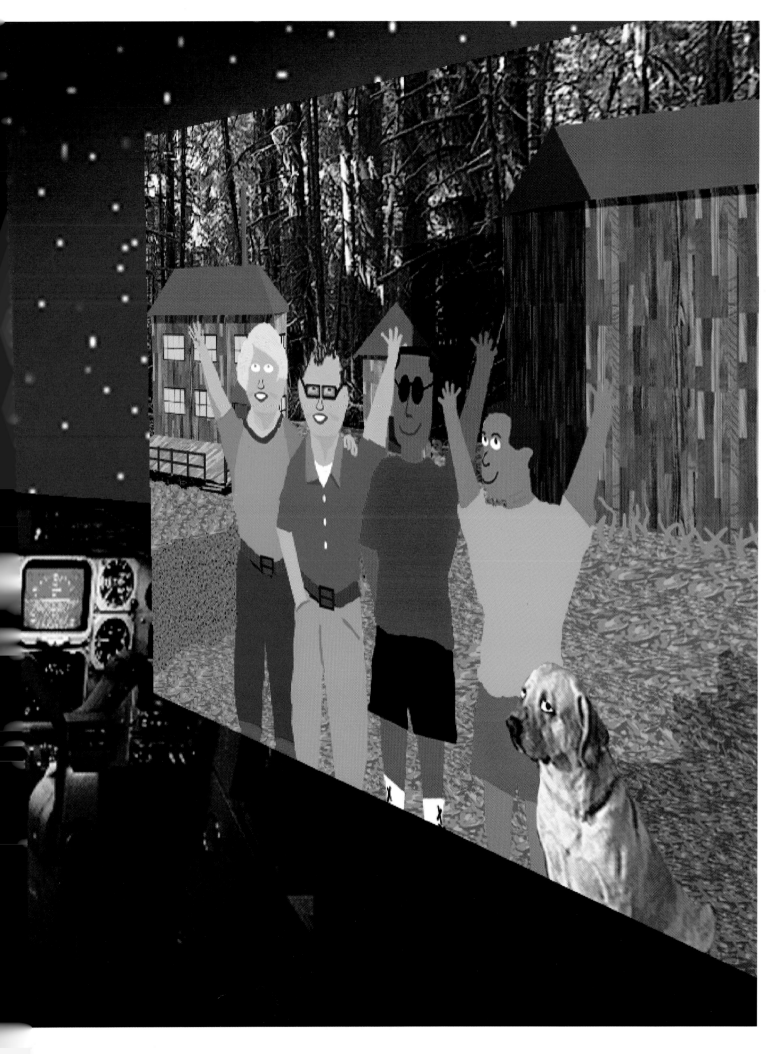

She focused the viewer on her friends, and watched them wave goodbye. "Good, no boxes. Even Juan's box is gone. I'm glad that is taken care of. I like having friends who aren't boxed in."

The End
<u>Moral</u>

Why live in a box when you can live anywhere in the world? Take it from Barb and Mr. Filmore, always read, and then read more.

Through Reading, Anyone Can do Anything.